arvelous Martin ™
Neighborhood P.I.

The Freckle-Faced Bully

by
Vincent Alexandria

MARIMBA BOOKS
An imprint of Hudson Publishing Group, LLC.
P. O. Box 5306
East Orange, NJ 07019

MARVELOUS MARTIN—Neighborhood P.I. ™: The Freckle-Faced Bully
Text copyright © 2010 by Vincent Alexandria.

All Marimba Book titles, imprints, and distributed lines are available at
special quantity discounts for bulk purchases for sales promotions, premiums,
fund-raising, and educational or institutional use.

Special book excerpts or customized printings can also be created to fit special needs.
For details, write or phone the office of the Marimba Books special sales manager.
Marimba Books, P. O. Box 5306, East Orange, NJ 07019
973 672-7701
www.marimbabooks.com

ISBN-13: 978-1-60349-013-9   ISBN-10: 1-60349-013-2
First Marimba Books Printing January 2010

10 9 8 7 6 5 4

Printed in the USA

MARVELOUS MARTIN—Neighborhood P.I. ™
is a creation of Vincent Alexandria. All rights reserved.

Cover design by 2nd Chapter

Marvelous Martin Neighborhood P.I.:

The Freckle-Faced Bully

This book is dedicated to my children
Preston, Randi, Royce, Azia and Nia.

—V.A.

"Marvelous" Martin Mitchell is a ten-year-old neighborhood Private Investigator. If something is missing or stolen, if a bully is taking advantage of a weaker person, Marvelous Martin is on the case. He's good at solving mysteries and usually gets paid for his sleuthing, too. Martin is very smart, but he is a normal kid who likes playing baseball, basketball and hanging out with his dog, Dutch. He also has a five-piece band called "Martin and the Marvels." Join an adventure with Marvelous Martin as he takes on **the Freckle-Faced Bully**.

Chapter 1
Tree House

My name is Martin Mitchell and I'm ten years old. My friends call me Marvelous Martin because I am the neighborhood Private Investigator. I got the name Marvelous from Ms. Crenshaw who lives up the street. When she lost her poodle, Precious, she asked me if I could help find her pet.

I knew that she rarely let the dog out of the house without a leash, so my dog, Dutch, and I looked around the apartment building where she lived. But we didn't see any trace of Precious. I asked Ms. Crenshaw what she had been doing earlier. She said she had been washing clothes. So Dutch and I went to the basement of the apartment building where the laundry room was located. There, sitting wagging her tail was

1

Precious. She jumped into my arms, and I brought her to Ms. Crenshaw. From that day on, Ms. Crenshaw would always tell me how marvelous I was. My friends started teasing me by calling me Marvelous and the name stuck.

Now, if something is lost or stolen, I'm on the case. I've solved cases of stolen watches, lunches, coats, and tennis shoes. I'm not a genius or anything. I use time and patience to solve my cases. I ask good fact-finding questions, then use the process of elimination. People are basically creatures of habit, and if you set up the same scenario, people will do the same thing. Like my dad says, "A thief is always a thief."

Take the stolen lunch case. I asked my mom to make me a special lunch with chicken, apple pie, potato salad, a Snickers candy bar, and a biscuit. I usually buy lunch from the cafeteria, but I wanted something different to eat. I talked about my lunch so much on the playground, everybody wanted to share it.

When I returned from the playground my lunch was gone. Someone had stolen it. Other students said their lunches had also been stolen during the week. I set out to solve the case.

The next day, I brought my lunch again. But this time I had a plan. I went to a detective store the evening before and bought a bottle of invisible dye. The man who owned the store said that the dye could only be seen with a special light. The special light looked like a miniature flashlight. I bought it, too. That morning, I put on my rubber gloves and coated my lunch bag with the dye.

At 12:30, I checked my locker and sure enough, my lunch was gone. A few of my classmates told me they had seen Steve Hicks with my lunch. So when I saw him go into the bathroom, I went to confront him.

"I heard that you stole my lunch," I told him.

"What are you talking about, Martin? I didn't do any such thing."

I could see the Snickers bar sticking out of his pocket.

"Well, what's that in your pocket? I had a Snickers in my lunch bag."

"I bought this candy from the store. I don't know what you're talking about."

I stared him down.

"Open your hands."

"Open my hands?!" he shot back. "Open my

hands for what?"

"Just do it."

Not knowing what my plan was, Steve opened both of his hands and held them out for me to see. I pulled the special light from my pocket and beamed it on Steve's hands. Both had purple dye on them. Steve was busted.

I took Steve to the principal's office where he confessed that he had indeed been stealing lunches. As punishment, the principal made Steve stay after school for three whole weeks.

So you can say I'm good at solving difficult cases. Sometimes I get paid. I usually accept whatever the client can afford, which has been anything from two dollars to ten bucks.

I watch a lot of detective shows on television with my dad. A detective can learn a lot from those shows. You guessed it. I want to work in law enforcement like my father, who's a detective with the city police department. But I want to be a Private Investigator.

"To serve and protect. I keep the community safe." That's what my dad always says.

Well, I help keep my neighborhood safe. I keep my school safe, too. If a bully picks on someone, the kid being picked on usually comes to me. And like I said, I'm no genius, but I am creative. I use different methods to find a solution. Sometimes, I uncover a secret the bully has and threaten to make it public if he or she doesn't stop the bullying. Or I might find a bigger kid and pay him to scare off the bully. It's a pretty cool business. I've already made more than sixty-six dollars. I keep my money hidden in my tree house, which serves as my office.

I'm in my tree house now. It is a beautiful day. The sun is shining, the birds are chirping and I feel marvelous. I just finished counting the money I'm saving to buy a new bike. It is a titanium, twenty-one speed, silver-blue, Huffy mountain bike. It costs one hundred thirty-five dollars.

I glance over at my friend Jasmine's house. Every day, I see her crazy doll staring back at me from her bedroom window, showing that big, goofy smile. His name is Mr. Bean and he reminds me of Mr. Potato Head. Mr. Bean wears a green hat, yellow glasses and has big wide eyes, pink ears, and blue shoes. He is a gift that Jasmine's father brought back from a trip to Ghana, West

Africa. Jasmine has always loved that doll, especially since her father died last year. I, on the other hand, really don't like Mr. Bean at all. Jasmine doesn't understand why I don't like her favorite doll, and neither do I. He just bugs me for some reason. I guess it's just one of those things.

I shake my head at the crazy doll and smile as I think about Jasmine. She sort of looks up to me like a big brother and asks me questions all the time. A familiar voice below makes me look down. Below my tree house I see little snaggle-toothed, eight-year-old Freddy Freeman crying his heart out. I let him come up into the tree house and hand him a tissue so he can dry his eyes. Dutch looks up at him. Both Dutch and I are curious. What is wrong with my friend?

"What's up, Freddy? What are the tears about?" I ask.

Little Freddy blows his small button nose and his light brown face turns red as he frowns.

"Freckle-faced Mark Beeks took my yellow bike and won't give it back," he cries pitifully. "I need you to get it back for me. I got money."

He pushes several wrinkled bills toward me. I push the snotty bills back and smile at my unhappy client.

"You don't have to pay me until I get your bike back," I tell him.

Freddy Freeman is small for his age. He has big ears and very large feet that are two sizes bigger than mine, and I wear an eight. His eyes are small and light brown and he has sandy brown hair that's curly. I pull an empty folder from my file cabinet and write, "Case of Freddy Freeman and the Freckle-Faced Bully!" on it. I grab a red lollipop from the cabinet and hand it to little Freddy Freeman as he plays with the money in his hands.

"You just sit tight little fella. I'm on the case."

I close the file, tie my sneakers, and let Dutch lick at my fingers. I know he's hungry. Dutch is always hungry. He'll eat just about anything.

I look over at Freddy Freeman and Freddy gives me a cherry-colored, snaggle-toothed grin. I give him another tissue and squirt a dab of antibacterial gel on his hands. After blowing his nose, he rubs his hands together with the gel on them.

"It kills germs, Freddy," I say. "I don't want

either of us to get sick over this," I say, only half joking.

I grab a note pad and sit Freddy on a milk crate.

"Okay Freddy, tell me exactly what happened."

Freddy pulls the sucker out of his mouth, takes a deep breath and licks his lips.

"I was riding down Buck O'Neil Boulevard early this morning, near Slimy Sam's Junkyard. That's when that big bully jumped in front of me. He balled up a big fat fist, held it to my nose, and told me to give up my bike or he would punch me in the face."

Little Freddy looks down at his big feet and I feel sorry for him. I have had my own experiences with bullies. Just the thought of them makes me upset.

"Did he hit you?" I ask.

Little Freddy shakes his head.

"Naw, I didn't want to get hit, so I gave him my bike and ran all the way over here to you!"

I want to laugh, but I know that it would hurt little Freddy's feelings. So I bite my lip and keep

9

my face as straight as I can. Freddy pops the cherry lollipop back in his mouth and sulks.

"My mom just got me that bike. She gets back in town in two days and I need to have it back at the house by then or I'm gonna be in big trouble."

Now I feel really bad for Freddy, but he is not giving me much time to get his bike back. I have less than about forty-eight hours to solve this case and save Freddy's behind.

"So, where was the last place you saw this bully with your new bike?" I ask.

Little Freddy frowns again. He pulls the lollipop from his mouth once more.

"Mark was riding my bike into his uncle's junkyard," he answers.

I get up and help little Freddy to his feet.

"Okay, we're going to need some help with this one. I'll check out Mark at school tomorrow. He's in my math class. I'll figure out the best way to get your bike back. You can bet on that."

Freddy grins that snaggled-tooth smile and we shake hands.

"Okay, Marvelous Martin. I'm counting on you."

I help Freddy out of the tree house and the two of us stand in my yard.

"No worries, little man. I'll take care of everything."

Chapter 2
Meet the Bully

When I arrive at St. Benedict's Middle School the next morning, I look for Mark Beeks in the hallway. It doesn't take me long to find him. I just follow the ruckus. The freckle-faced bully is near my locker taunting Darion Thornbeck. Darion is a tall, slender, shy kid who stays to himself. He's a true science wiz, too. Mark has Darion pinned to his locker, which is three lockers down from mine.

I enter my combination and keep an eye on what's going on. When Darion tries to wiggle away from his locker, his face turning red with frustration, Mark pushes him hard against the locker door.

BAM!

I know the impact of his back banging the locker door hurts because Darion grimaces.

"Mark, leave him alone!"

The words just slip from my mouth without warning. I have no idea how the brave command came out, but the freckle-faced bully releases Darion. He walks toward me with his nose scrunched up and a scowl on his face. A crowd gathers quickly, anticipating a fight. But a fight is the last thing that I want.

Mark's face is close to mine and I can smell his foul breath.

"You need to mind your own business Martin, you nerd!"

"I admit that I'm smart, but, a nerd I'm not."

As Mark shouts, his chest puffs up and his hands turn into tight big fists. "You want a piece of me?"

I take a step back. "Not exactly."

I see Principal Skinner down the hall heading our way and I breathe a sigh of relief.

"I don't want to get detention," I answer nervously.

Mark spots the principal, too. The freckle-faced bully eyes me and frowns.

"We have issues now, Martin. You owe me lunch. See you after third period," he says, and pushes me in the head with his finger.

I don't want to fight this large kid but I don't want to buy him lunch, either.

"I don't think that's going to happen, Mark. But I will see you in math class," I answer.

My friends and members of my band, John Ashford, Victor Vargas, Gino Melvin, and Jimmy Young, arrive at my locker about the same time Principal Skinner does.

Ash has been playing keyboards since he was four years old. He keeps his blond hair neatly trimmed. Victor plays guitar and always wears a Carlos Santana T-shirt. His shiny black hair hangs to his shoulders. Jimmy is our drummer. He wears braids most of the time. Gino is the shortest of the group. He plays saxophone.

"Is there a problem here, young men?" Principal Skinner asks.

"No sir, Mr. Skinner," Mark quickly answers before I can open my mouth. He stares at me, daring me to say anything different.

I hesitate and respond with a forced smile.

"Everything is great, sir."

Principal Skinner looks at us and at the other students hanging around, trying to figure out what is going on.

"Mark, you know you can't afford another detention. One more and you're suspended. You all get to class. There are only three minutes before the bell rings."

"Yes, sir," we all say in unison as we hurry to our various classes.

Mark Beeks is seated one person across from me. Les Brown sits between us. Les leans over toward me.

"What you get on your test, Martin?" he asks.

I show him my paper. "I got a ninety-seven. What about you?" I ask. He smiles and points to the big red ninety-six in the upper right corner of his test.

"Good job," I say. We tap fists to congratulate each other. Then he leans closer to me.

"The bully got a fifty-six."

Mark overhears Les and gives Les' chair a quick kick. Some of the students who see the incident start to laugh. Ms. Crabwood, our teacher, comes over to us.

"Is there a problem?" she asks as she taps her foot on the hardwood floor, waiting

16

for an answer.

As always, Mark speaks first.

"These two . . . " Mark catches himself before he can say something Ms. Crabwood wouldn't like. Then he composes himself.

"They were making jokes about my test score," he explains.

Les' mouth drops open. So does mine.

"We were just curious. We never teased him, Ms. Crabwood," I say.

Mark is usually pretty good in math. He seems to have difficulties only with word problems.

Ms. Crabwood places one hand on Les' desk and the other on my desk.

"Gentlemen, we need to be concerned only with our own grades," she tells us.

I look Mark's way and he makes a fist so I can see it but no one else can.

"Mr. Mitchell, I'm surprised at you and at Mr. Brown. I expect all of us to respect each other. We do have that understanding, do we not, students?"

"Yes, ma'am."

I turn to face Mark.

"I'm sorry, Mark," I apologize, hoping my gesture will put an end to his anger.

Mark smirks and rolls his eyes, pointing to the clock while Les apologizes.

I know I'm not going to fight Mark. But I've got to find some way to get little Freddy's bike back. Maybe I should try to understand why Mark is the way he is. There has to be a reason for his anger. I know it isn't me. He seems so unhappy all the time.

I heard he's been living with his uncle since his parents died in a car accident three years ago. His uncle owns a junkyard not far from my house. Some kids say he got his mean streak because he was forced to live with an uncle and because his uncle is so mean. I've never seen his uncle, but I heard he is a big man. I know kids can run a rumor mill faster than a hamster can turn a wheel. So, I think I should try to get the real facts myself. That's what a good detective does. One thing is for sure, however. You never see Mark hanging around with anyone. So it doesn't surprise me that kids would start rumors about him. He's such a loner.

When the bell rings to end class, I quickly head to the hallway to meet Ash, Jimmy, Gino, and Victor. I rush them into the lunchroom and we get in line to get our food.

I look over my shoulder often, not knowing when Mark Beeks plans to show his face and start trouble. I don't see him anywhere in the cafeteria. Maybe he's skipping lunch or had a sudden streak of kindness and let our disagreement pass. Victor touches me on the shoulder and I jump.

"What's your problem? Why are you so nervous?"

Gino quickly answers, like he can't wait to spread the news to the guys.

"Mark the Bully is after him 'cause he took up for Darion in the hallway this morning. Marvelous was great," Gino says admiringly as he pats me on the shoulder.

Victor looks at me and Gino suspiciously. "No way!"

"Yes way!" Gino nods his head, smiling proudly.

I give Gino a long cold stare.

"What, dude?" he asks innocently as he shrugs his shoulders.

Gino calls everyone dude.

"Marvelous, the hero. When did you get to be so brave?" Ash laughs and shakes his head.

I roll my eyes at him and move forward in the lunch line.

"You guys know I wasn't trying to start a fight, right?" I tell them.

"I hope not," quips Ash. "Mark would beat the snot out of you. He's got you by at least fifty pounds. I just saw him in the boy's bathroom taking money from one of the sixth graders. He's one bad dude. What's your plan, Martin?"

"I don't know. I can't afford to get into any trouble in school. My parents would kill me."

Jimmy pushes me forward in line.

"Marvelous, you have to stand up to this guy or he'll be bullying you for the rest of the school year. Man-up. Don't let him push you around."

Gino eyes my tray and changes the subject.

"Dude, you gonna eat that fruit cocktail?"

"Aw, man, I'm on Mark's hit list and all you can do is think about food," I complain. "Dang, Gino."

Still, I hand him my fruit cup and grab a carton of chocolate milk from the food counter. We laugh and keep moving through the lunch line to get our spaghetti and meatballs, salad, and garlic sticks. We show our lunch cards to the cafeteria cashier and head to our favorite table. When we reach our table, Gino nudges me in the side with his elbow.

20

"Martin, have you decided what you're going to do about Mark?"

I place my tray on the table.

"Nah, not yet," I answer.

"Well, you better think quickly, because big bully Mark is coming. Look to your left," he warns.

I take a deep breath to calm myself and gather my thoughts as fast as I can. I take a seat with my friends and center my tray in front of me. Mark approaches and when he arrives, he towers over me.

"So, where's my lunch, nerd?" His massive arms are folded in front of his heaving body. The bully's frame blocks the light that shines from the fluorescent bulbs above us. Ashford gets up from his place at the table, and I motion for him to sit down. No need for him to get in trouble on my behalf.

I look up at the big kid.

"Look, Mark. Yes, you are one of the biggest kids in school and a lot bigger than me. I know you like picking on people smaller than you are. But unlike the other kids, I'm not scared of you. If you are that hungry and don't have lunch, you can have mine. But this is a one-time deal. I'm not getting into trouble because of you, at school or anywhere else. It's not worth it, so you can take that bully stuff somewhere else."

Mark's face starts turning red and his cheeks fill with air. He pushes my head so hard, it almost hits the table.

"I knew you wouldn't fight, nerd." With that, he pushes my tray on my lap and storms off.

The spaghetti and meatballs spill over my legs. Kids who saw the incident start to laugh at me and get up from their seats to see what damage Mark has caused. Jimmy, Gino, Victor, and Ashford want to go after him, but I insist they stay at the table and let it ride. I clean up the mess and go to the bathroom to get the red sauce off my blue jeans the best I can.

I use water, soap, and paper towels to clean my jeans and the hand dryer to blow dry my pants and head to my next class. I'm proud of myself for not fighting and also for standing up to Mark Beeks.

Marvelous Martin
Neighborhood P.I.

Chapter 3
Scouting the Enemy

After school, I decide not to walk home with my friends. Instead, I follow Mark Beeks to his house. I guess you can call it undercover work.

It's funny, most kids walk in a group of two or more, but Mark walks alone. It seems like he takes pride in pushing aside kids who are in his path as he rumbles down the sidewalk. The guy is truly mean. I lag behind, just far enough to go unnoticed. If he sees me, I'm sure I'll have to fight him or come up with one of the best excuses ever created. It seems as if he's stomping down the street instead of walking. It's a funny thing to watch.

The backpack that Mark carries seems as small as a wallet across his huge back. His hands are dug deep into his pockets and his head is craned forward.

I start to feel sorry for the kid. He must be terribly lonely.

It's about an eight block walk to the junkyard where Mark lives. As he approaches the gate, I see two big dogs inside the tall fence. They start barking when they see Mark. Mark opens the gate and enters the yard. I slow down and duck behind a tree so he won't see me. Mark pats the two dogs and then they all disappear inside a white trailer. I wait a few minutes, cross the street and head home.

Chapter 4

Slimy Sam's Junkyard

As soon as I get home, I call Ash, Jimmy, Victor, Gino, and little Freddy Freeman, and ask them to meet me so we can get Freddy's bike back. I even decide to let Jasmine tag along. Mark Beeks is a big kid with an attitude problem. I can use everyone's help on this case.

We gather on Satchel Paige Boulevard, near the junkyard. The street was named in honor of Satchel Paige, who played for the Kansas City Monarchs in the Negro Baseball League when Buck O'Neil was the manager. Satchel Paige was the oldest player to ever play Major League Baseball. He had one of the fastest fastballs and one of the highest strike-out records ever. It's cool to have my neighborhood streets named after famous athletes like them.

So, here I stand with all my friends except Jimmy, getting ready for this big caper. Gino looks as if he has gained several pounds since lunch. He's chewing bubble gum and has packages of beef jerky stuck in one of his back pockets.

"Jimmy will be along in a minute," he says.

I give a "what's-up" nod to the group and begin to tell them about my visit to Mark's place.

I stop when I see Jimmy coming. He has an unfamiliar girl wearing braces with him. She hangs close to Jimmy. Everybody is wondering who this pretty new girl is.

Finally, Jimmy gets the idea.

"Hey, everybody. Meet my cousin Azia Marie. She's from Dallas, Texas. She's here for the weekend and my pops said I couldn't leave the house without her."

"You know you wanted me to come with you, old silly boy," Azia Marie blurts out. She punches Jimmy on the arm.

Azia Marie smiles at everyone allowing her braces to gleam.

"Ouch, that hurt! You play way too much!" Jimmy whines as he takes a step away from his cute cousin. We all laugh at him.

Azia Marie has long braids, big eyes, and brown sugar-colored skin. She's a little taller than Jimmy, and seems friendly enough.

She looks at me. "I heard you have a band, Marvelous Martin. I play percussion and would love to play with you guys."

Jimmy steps forward, looking her up and down. "I'm the drummer in this group. So we'll take a rain check, okay?"

She rolls her eyes. "If you're good, it shouldn't be a problem."

"Ooooohhhhhh," we all say in unison, impressed.

Jimmy rolls his eyes and responds, "Well, since you're that good, go play for Jay-Z then."

Azia and Jimmy eye each other.

Gino steps in between them.

"At this rate, we'll never find out who's better. Are we going to get this kid's bike back or what? We're wasting time and we are supposed to have practice today," he reminds us.

Jimmy shoves his hands into his pockets. "We'll finish this later," he says to his cousin.

Azia Marie winks at him.

"You think?" She smiles and Jimmy shakes his head in grief.

Little Freddy Freeman stands patiently next to me and Ash. Gino looks over at the junkyard and then looks at little Freddy.

"Dude, you sure you want to go in there looking for your bike? It could take all day in that big old place."

Freddy nods his head.

"I have to get my bike back by the time my mom gets home. I don't care how long it takes. I have to get that bike!"

"Oh, you're so brave," Azia Marie jokes with a smile. But Freddy just stares. He doesn't think it's funny.

We cross the street and stand at the entrance of the huge junkyard.

"You think Mark is here?" Gino asks.

I look around and see the big dirty white trailer sitting off to the left. "If he is, he's probably in there," I say, gesturing with my hand.

Jasmine grabs my arm and points to a big sign that reads "Beware of Dogs."

"Martin, I got a bad feeling about this," she warns, clutching Mr. Bean close to her.

All of our eyes scan the premises for any signs of the guard dogs.

"I think he keeps them in that trailer. That's where he took them when—"

"I forgot you have been here already," Jimmy says, cutting me off. "Maybe you should have

brought Dutch along."

Freddy's eyes grow as big as I've ever seen them.

"Dogs or no dogs! I have to get my b-b-bike!"

"So, what is the plan, detective?" Victor inquires of me. "What do we do?"

"We spread out and look under these cars first. We can cover more ground if we separate. Holla if you see it."

Everyone agrees. We all walk slowly through the entrance of the junkyard. It's filled with old beat-up and wrecked cars, trucks and buses. We only get a few yards when the door to the trailer bursts open.

"What are you guys doing here?" Mark Beeks asks with a growl.

His body takes up the whole doorway. I can see why Little Freddy gave up his bike. Mark is truly a big, scary guy. We all look at each other for an answer. I think about running away just as little Freddy did. But I put my fears aside. I promised to help Freddy get his bike back. Besides, I'm a detective. I've gotta figure this out.

"Are you guys stupid, dumb, or crazy?" Mark Beeks barks. "What do you want?"

"Nobody's scared of you, big head boy!" Azia

Marie shouts with an attitude. She puts her hands on her waist and starts toward the bully. Jimmy stops her by grabbing her arm.

Mark's face turns red.

"What? You wanna start something, girl?!"

I step up hesitantly, not wanting to make things worse than they already are.

"Mark, we want the bike you took from Freddy Freeman. You give it back and we're out of here."

Mark starts to laugh and his whole body shakes.

"I don't know what you're talking about. I didn't take any bike."

Little Freddy Freeman pushes his way up front.

"Yes, you did too take my bike! You said you were gonna hit me if I didn't give it to you, you big bully!"

Freddy sticks his tongue out at Mark then quickly darts behind me.

"Mark, you're going to get the kid in trouble. You've had your fun. Give the kid back his bike," Ash tells the bully.

Mark takes a step down the trailer stairs.

"I ain't giving anything back. You guys better

get out of here before I let my uncle's dogs out. They don't play," he warns, smiling devilishly.

I step forward, not really knowing what propelled me to do so.

"We're not leaving until we get Freddy's bike back. We'll look around this junkyard all day until we find it. There's nothing you can do about it!"

A big grin spreads across Mark's face. I know it's not a good sign.

"Oh, yeah?" Mark yells. "Oh, yeah?"

"Yeah!" we all say in unison. I guess everyone is feeling brave because we outnumber Mark.

Mark nods his big head and shakes his fist at us. He storms back up the stairs and into the trailer, slamming the door shut. We cheer for a few seconds, reveling in our success. Then we spread out again and begin to search for little Freddy's bike.

Suddenly, the door to the trailer flies open again. Mark stands in the doorway with two big, barking German shepherds. He has a leash on each.

"I'm gonna count to three and y'all better get to running," Mark screams. "ONE! TWO! THREE!" He releases the dogs.

Chapter 5
Run for Your Life

We run as fast as our legs can carry us. I have Jasmine by the hand, pulling her along. We can't make it out of the yard. The dogs will catch us if we try.

"Ha! Ha! Ha! Ha! Ha! Ha!" We hear Mark laughing.

I make it to an old blue SUV, hop on the bumper and pull Jasmine up with me. We scramble to the hood of the vehicle and climb to the top. I look to see where my friends are. Thank goodness I find them all standing on the hoods and tops of SUVs and pickup trucks, too. The dogs run from one car to another, barking and trying to reach us. But they can't. Luckily, we all managed to find tall vehicles.

I catch my breath and try to think of a way out of this scary situation. I look at the old

vehicles around me. The only one that seems to have windows is an old gray van. There is a small yellow car between the SUV I am on and the gray van.

"Gino, do you still have that beef jerky?" I yell to my friend, who always seems to be hungry.

"Yeah, I still have the beef jerky. But dude, how can you think about eating at a time like this?"

Gino clutches the two packages of beef jerky that are still in his back pocket. The two dogs continue to bark furiously as they try to leap onto the SUVs. I look for Mark, but I don't see him. It looks as if he has left us to the dogs.

"I need the beef jerky," I tell Gino.

"I need it, too."

"Look, Gino, I have an idea. You can always get some more."

"Man, why do I have to give my food away?" Gino protests over the dogs' barking. He pulls the beef jerky from his pocket. The two dogs bark furiously at Gino, Ash and Freddie.

"Aw, come on. We'll get you a whole box of that stuff," Ash tells Gino. He is sitting on a truck with Gino and Freddy Freeman. "Our detective friend says he has an idea."

Ash grabs the beef jerky from Gino's hand.

"Here, Martin. Catch."

"Be careful, Ash. If we drop the beef jerky on the ground, my plan is a wrap," I warn.

"I play baseball, remember?"

"Yeah, I remember, Ash. Throw the beef jerky."

Ash tosses both packages of beef jerky perfectly. I catch them and push them into my front pocket. The first part of my plan is done. Now for the second part.

I have to get to the gray van. I jump on top of the trunk of the yellow car and crawl onto the top to make my way to the hood.

The gray van is now in front of me. It is too tall for me to leap onto. I will have to stand on the bumper to get enough leverage to reach the hood. But if I get to the ground, the two dogs will surely get me. And I can't stand on the bumper too long. The dogs will get to me there, too.

"Hey, Jimmy," I call out. "Make a lot of noise so you can draw the dogs' attention." The pickup that Jimmy and Victor are on is the farthest from me. If they can get the dogs focused on their truck, I can make it to the van.

As soon as Jimmy and Victor start yelling and beating on the truck, the two dogs scurry over. The shepherds circle the truck, looking for a way to get on top.

Now, I have my chance. I jump down from the yellow car and onto the ground.

"Hurry, Marv, before they see you!" Ash warns.

I get up on the back bumper of the van.

I hear the dogs barking like crazy. The barking seems to be getting closer. And it is closer.

"They're coming, Marv! They're coming!" Jimmy shouts to me.

"Hurry, Martin! I don't want those dogs to get you," a frightened Jasmine screams. *I don't, either,* I think to myself.

As the dogs get even closer, I'm thinking that they must really believe they can get me. But not this time.

I scramble quickly to the top of the van and look down at the barking dogs.

Ash says, "That was close, Marvelous."

"You got that right."

I crawl toward the front of the van, hoping that the doors aren't locked. All of the windows are rolled up, so that's good news. I reach over to the passenger's side to check the door. It is locked. One of the dogs leaps up and almost catches my hand. I pull away and move quickly to the driver's side before the dogs can circle around and see what I'm doing. I reach down to the handle of the door and squeeze. The door releases and I pull it wide open. The two dogs scamper to the driver's side.

Don't they ever get tired of barking?

Now, for the rest of my plan. I open one of the packages of beef jerky, break off two small pieces and throw them to the ground near the van door. The dogs sniff the pieces of jerky and quickly snap them up. The hungry beasts look around for more. I break off two more pieces and throw them near the van door again.

One dog gets both pieces this time. I open the other package of jerky, break it in half and throw both pieces and the remainder of the first piece inside the van, all the way to the passenger's seat. The two German shepherds leap into the van after the meat. I reach for the door of the van and slam it shut. The dogs are now trapped inside.

"We did it! We did it!" Ash jumps down from the car and pats me on the back. The others scramble down from their perches, too.

"Now, we can find the bike," I tell the group.

"Let's spread out like we started to do before

we were rudely interrupted. Search beneath every car."

We all go off in different directions. It's not long before Gino rushes back to me, wheeling a yellow bike.

"I found it, Marvelous. You were right. It was hidden beneath one of those cars."

Freddy Freeman rushes over, beaming from ear to ear. "You got it! You got it!"

He grabs the bike from Gino and does a dance.

"Well, Freddy, my boy, we got your bike." I tell him.

"We better get out of here before something else happens," Victor cautions. He is right.

We start walking out of the junkyard. Everyone is happy. Little Freddy rides his newly recovered bike. I look back at the trailer to see if the bully has reappeared. He is nowhere in sight. We're in the clear.

Just as we get to the gate, Mark Beeks jumps out in front of us and blocks our exit. Where did he come from?

"And where do you think you are going with my bike?" he snarls.

Chapter 6
What a Day!

Mark stands in front of us huffing and puffing like someone stole the ham sandwich from his lunch box. His nostrils flare, his hands are balled into fists and his baseball cap is turned backwards on his head. And he's grinding his teeth.

What a day! We've been in this junkyard looking for little Freddy Freeman's stolen bike for what seems like all afternoon. We've been chased by two vicious dogs that would have shredded us to pieces if it weren't for Gino's beef jerky. Now, big-head Mark Beeks is trying to trap us in this junkyard. My friends look at me for direction.

"What did you guys do with my dogs?" Mark asks, pumping his fist in the air.

I point to the gray van.

41

"They're over there having dinner." I smile but Mark doesn't see anything funny about it. He frowns at my cleverness.

"Wipe that smile off your face before I wipe it off for you," he threatens.

Now *I'm* mad. I take three large steps toward the bully.

"Mark, we can do this the hard way or the easy way." I point to little Freddy Freeman's yellow bike.

"This is Freddy's bike. You took it from him and now we're taking it back. You can just let us out of here and we can call it a day, or we can call the cops." I reach in my pocket and hold up my cell phone to show him I mean business.

Mark stands firm. My friends gather around me and we all wait to see how this will play out. Mark takes two steps toward me and we all take two steps back.

"I'll just tell the cops you guys broke into my uncle's junkyard and that y'all are trespassing. I'll tell them you had the bike when you broke in." Mark smiles. He's feeling smart right now.

I think about what Mark has just said and he does have a point. We did force our way into the junkyard. I ponder our next move and can only come to one conclusion.

"Get him!" I yell.

We all rush the freckle-faced bully and tackle him to the ground. I sit on his right leg. Ash grabs an arm. Gino takes his left leg. Everyone has a part of him pinned to the ground. Mark struggles, trying to get free, but he can't. And then to our amazement, the big bully starts to cry.

"You just wait, Martin. I'm going to get each and every one of you guys. You better let me get up," he demands. We start to laugh.

"Well, Mark, until you calm down and take back what you said, we're not letting you up," I inform him.

Little Freddy Freeman sits on the big bully's stomach and looks him in the face.

"That's what you get for messing with us. You aren't so bad now, are you?" he teases.

Mark struggles but still can't get free. His lower lip trembles with anger.

"You just wait, you little nerd. I'm gonna get you."

"Y'all get up off me right now and I promise

not to beat up the girls."

"Dude, you got serious issues," Gino says, frowning and shaking his head in disgust.

As I sit on Mark's huge leg, I look him directly in the face. Maybe I can talk some sense into that big head.

"Mark, we can end this now if you apologize to us and promise to stop bullying people." I put more pressure on his leg as I speak.

"Ouch!" he yells. "I'm not stopping anything. Y'all can't sit here all day. Just know when you let me up, I'm gonna get you."

He has a point.

"Let's just beat the crap out of him," Azia Marie says. She smacks her fist into her hand for emphasis.

"If we do that, we stoop to his level," I say.

Victor, who is sitting on Mark's right arm, turns to me.

"Mark is right. We can't sit here on him all day. We have to do something. I'm getting hungry."

"Amen to that!" Gino adds. "You gave those stupid dogs my beef jerky. And now I'm hungry after all this work."

"I know what we can do!" Jasmine says

confidently as she clutches Mr. Bean. "We can tie him up and throw him in the van with the dogs."

Jimmy rolls his eyes at Jasmine.

"Little girl, you watch way too much TV. You're dangerous!"

"We can't do that, Jasmine. We don't want to hurt him. Besides, if we do that the dogs would get out," I explain.

"Well, he didn't care about those dogs hurting us. Why should we care about him?"

"Because, Jasmine, we are not like Mark. We don't bully people or try to hurt them. Friends look out for each other, not try to hurt each other."

"He's not our friend!" little Freddy Freeman jumps in.

I look at Mark lying there defeated.

"He can be our friend if he wants to. Everybody, get up off him. We know what friendship is and we stand together. So Mark, if you want to fight us, you have to fight us all."

Victor, Gino, Azia Marie, Freddy, Ash, Jimmy, Jasmine, and I get up and dust ourselves off. Mark dusts himself off, too. Then he balls both hands into fists and starts toward us.

At that moment, a light-blue tow truck rumbles into the junkyard and stops right in front of us. A big man, more than six feet tall, leaps out. He has a salt-and-pepper beard and is wearing a blue Kansas City Royals baseball cap. His large muscles look as if they will burst from the shirt that's trying to hold them in.

"What's going on here?" he asks, studying us carefully.

We all look at each other and then at Mark. Mark looks at us and then at the man.

"Well, answer me, Mark. Who are these kids and why are they here?"

Mark doesn't seem so tough anymore. I notice that his hands are no longer balled into fists. His shoulders are slumped and he looks at the ground as if he expects it to answer.

All my friends notice how subdued Mark is now and they start to snicker. But I suddenly feel sorry for Mark. I see how lonely he really is. I step forward to meet the stranger.

"We are his friends, sir. We just came over to see how he is doing and to see if he can come to hear our band, the Marvels, practice." Obviously, I am lying.

My friends' mouths all fly wide open.

They can't believe what I have just said. I pull little Freddy Freeman closer to me before he can say anything different. Freddy frowns at me as he grabs the handles of his yellow bike.

Mark turns to me and for the first time, I see a smile on his face.

The man rubs his beard with his large hands and stares at us.

"Is this true, Mark?"

Mark looks at me. I smile and nod.

"Yes, Uncle Sam. I guess so," he answers hesitantly.

"You got your reading assignment done? You know you're flunking reading and need to get your work done."

"I'll help him with his work just as soon as we finish practice, sir," I volunteer. "I'm real good at reading and I'd love to help Mark get his grades up."

Mark's uncle eyes me, tilting his head to the side like he's trying to figure out who I am.

"What's your name?"

"Martin Mitchell, but my friends and family call me Marvelous," I respond as the big man looks me up and down.

"Oh, you're Detective Mitchell's boy, huh? I

thought you looked familiar."

Mark's mouth flies wide open when he hears "Detective Mitchell." His hands shoot up to his head and holds it in disbelief.

"Yes, sir, I am," I answer Mark's uncle.

"Looks like you got some good friends, Mark. Now, you run in and get your homework."

Mark dashes off. As soon as he enters the trailer, his uncle whispers to us.

"I've been hoping that Mark would make some good friends. He's such a loner. I always tell him that's not the way to be. He's still dealing with the loss of his Mom and Dad. I try to push him to be more outgoing, to make friends. Maybe I push too hard sometimes. Some kids are afraid of him because he's so big. But if they give him a break, they'll see that he's just a nice kid."

I nod my head politely, but my friends are dead silent.

Mark rushes out of the trailer carrying a small book bag. He is almost out of breath.

"Uncle Sam, I let the dogs out and put them in that van over there. You might want to let them out when you get a chance. I didn't want them to hurt my friends," Mark fibs.

Uncle Sam takes off his baseball cap and

scratches his balding head.

"You did what?" He looks over at the van and slaps his Royals cap on his thigh.

"Well, alright. I'll take care of them. Go on with your friends. And here, take this."

He reaches into his pocket and gives Mark a twenty-dollar bill.

"Gee, thanks, Uncle Sam."

Uncle Sam climbs back into the tow truck and waves to us as we leave the junkyard. As we step onto the sidewalk, we can see him park the truck next to the trailer.

My friends all seem somewhat confused by what has just happened. We walk without saying a word. Finally, Mark stops and breaks the silence.

"Hey guys, I'm sorry for what I did back there. You all could have ratted me out to my uncle if you wanted to. But you didn't. I appreciate that." He looks as if he really means what he has said.

"Yeah, we could have and you would have got in a whole lot of trouble, too, but we didn't," little Freddy Freeman says, rolling his eyes as he rides his yellow bike beside us.

Azia Marie steps up to Mark.

"You were really mean to us back there.

We didn't do anything to you to cause you to treat us that way."

"Yeah!" Jasmine adds, shaking her Mr. Bean doll at Mark.

Mark shoves his hands in his pockets.

"I said I was sorry," he says. He turns away. It looks as if he is going to go back home.

"Okay guys, ease up," I tell the group. "He said he was sorry. Let's give him a break, okay?"

"Yeah, it's all history now and I'm hungry," adds Gino.

"Dude, you owe me some beef jerky," he tells Mark. A smile returns to Mark's face.

"Hey, listen," I say. "I have ten bucks on me. Let's go over to Torri's Hotdog stand around the corner. I'm buying."

Everyone cheers.

"Marvelous Martin's paying for the hotdogs, but I'm buying the ice cream, chips, and soda," Mark offers.

I pat Mark on the back as we all head down the sidewalk.

"Mark, you're alright with me," I say to him as we turn the corner to Torri's.

"Thank you, Marvelous Martin. It's good to

have friends."

Little Freddy Freeman sits tall on his bike as we quicken our pace to get to our feast. He's whistling a song and after a few seconds we all recognize it. It's "Who Let the Dogs Out?"

Chapter 7

Another Case

I t's a bright sunny morning but I'm not quite ready to get out of bed. It has been two weeks since my pals and I befriended the big, freckle-faced former bully, Mark Beeks. Mark has been coming over to my tree house for tutoring in reading three days a week. And he is reading much better. I have him reading out loud like my mom and dad did with me. He is happy with his progress and so is his uncle. Mark even got a "B" on his last reading test.

I had Mark promise that he will read half an hour every day on his own. Given the hour of reading he does with me, he should be up to speed with our class in about a month or so. I'm happy to see Mark do well. He's really an okay guy. He has even made a few more friends at school.

Mark's uncle pays me five dollars a week to help Mark. I also have the five dollars little Freddy Freeman paid me for getting his bike back. I smile, because I'm that much closer to having enough money to buy the bike I've been saving for.

I finally force myself out of bed. I'm in the top bunk of a new bunk bed my parents just bought for me. I jump down and kneel to pat Dutch on the head. He's lying on the floor next to my bed as he always does.

Then I walk to the window and look out. Jasmine's window faces mine. Jasmine is probably still asleep, but I see that stupid doll staring at me like he does every morning. I hate that Mr. Bean. But as I stare at him in disgust, something seems funny. The doll doesn't look quite right. His green hat is stuck to his side. He has pink ears for feet. His blue shoes are on top of his head. What really makes me take notice is that big goofy smile is upside down. Jasmine would never allow that doll to look like that. She loves it too much.

I decide to find out what's wrong with Mr. Bean later and I get back in bed.

Under the covers, I close my eyes and try to fall asleep again, but that weird Mr. Bean doll won't let me rest. Having a messed-up Mr. Bean is just not like Jasmine. And as much as I can't stand the doll, and as much as Jasmine bugs me by following me all the time, she is my friend.

"You have to look out for Jasmine," I can hear my mom say. "You're like a big brother to her."

Mom knows that "big brother" title gets to me. I roll over and peek from under my sheet to look at the electronic alarm clock on my desk. It's not even 9 a.m., and already I have another case on my hands.